~ DEMI ~

KING MIDAS

THE GOLDEN TOUCH

MARGARET K. McELDERRY BOOKS
NEW YORK   LONDON   TORONTO   SYDNEY   SINGAPORE

LONG AGO the ancient Greeks believed their gods were in the sky and the winds, the seas and the mountains—in everything. The people prayed to the gods for wisdom and power, knowledge and generosity, and moderation in all their ways.

There reigned in Phrygia a king named Midas.
He was weak and ignorant, miserly and greedy. And
he didn't think he needed to pray to the gods at all.
Everything King Midas did was backward.

One day King Midas was asked to judge a music contest between the great god Apollo and the little god Pan.

The little god Pan had a snub nose and the horns, ears, and hooves of a goat. He was mischievous and tricky. He was a protector of shepherds and their flocks. He played little pipes of reeds in the woods and on the mountains.

Apollo was known throughout
the heavens and the earth as the
god of harmony and music.
A single note he sang
could put the whole
universe in order.

Apollo was so majestic
and beautiful, the other
gods called him "The
Shining One" and compared
him to the sun. Apollo was
so powerful that he could
inflict illness with his
bow and arrows.

The contest began, and Apollo played first.
His notes on the lyre were so pure and sweet,
they sang through the woods and fields.
Even the birds were silent
as they listened
to the beautiful
music.

Then it was Pan's turn. He blew shrill, discordant sounds on his pipes. All the geese flew out of the pond. Squirrels scurried up trees, and skunks hid in their holes.

Anybody with any sense would have given the prize to the great god Apollo. But King Midas did not have sense.

"Wonderful! Wonderful!"
applauded the king.
"I crown little Pan
the winner with
this laurel wreath!"

Of course, Apollo was
furious. "Someone who is
as stupid and tone deaf
as you should have ears
to match. From now on
you shall have donkey's ears!"

To his horror, King Midas found long, pointed, furry ears sprouting from his head.

King Midas was miserable.

The king grew his hair long and wrapped it around his ears, to hide them in case his crown ever fell off. But soon he had too much hair. He visited the royal barber, who snipped and clipped and was astonished to find his king had donkey's ears.

The barber knew he must keep the king's secret, but he found it very hard to do.

The barber ran to the River Pactolus and dug a deep hole in the sandy bank. Into this hole he whispered his secret: "King Midas has donkey's ears!" He covered the secret with sand and returned to the palace.

Reeds grew over the secret spot. The winds
whispered the question, "Who has donkey's
ears?" And from somewhere below
would come the answer:
"Midas the king!"

One summer evening Dionysus, the god of feasting and merriment, hosted a party in Phrygia. Long after the party ended, one guest remained, asleep in a rose patch. This was Silenus the Satyr. Half man, half animal, Silenus has a horse's tail, hooves, and ears.

King Midas's men found Silenus and tied him up with rose garlands. They put a rosy wreath on his head and brought him before the king.

King Midas was happy to entertain one such as he—a man with long, furry ears. So for many days the king and Silenus played together like children, until Silenus realized that Dionysus must be looking for him. King Midas took Silenus back to Dionysus.

In gratitude for the return of his charge, Dionysus said to King Midas, "Ask for anything you like and I will give it to you!"

King Midas's eyes grew round, and his heart grew cold. "I want everything I touch to turn to gold!"

Running from room to room, the king touched
all he could—and everything turned to gold.

"Granted," Dionysus said, and he departed with Silenus.

King Midas jumped and skipped
and hopped back to his palace.
The earth turned to gold
beneath his feet.

Soon the palace gleamed and shone like one hundred suns!
King Midas was the richest man in the world and he thought he was happy.

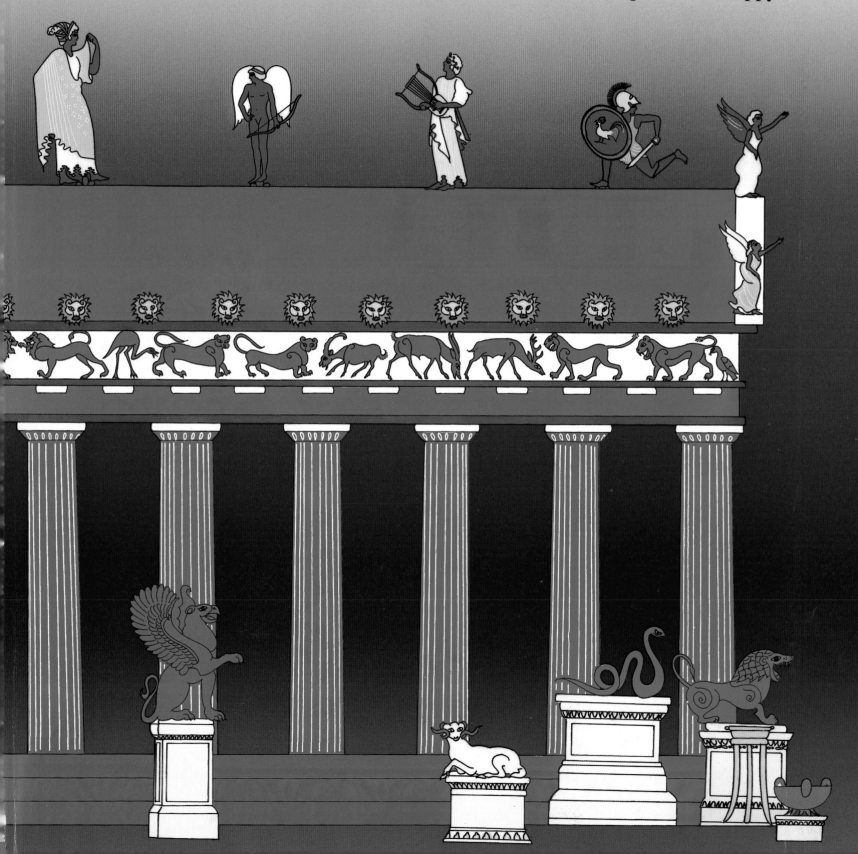

King Midas sat down to eat. The chair turned to gold.
The cup and dish turned to gold. The utensils
turned to gold.

He tried to drink, but the liquid was
a solid ribbon of gold.

His meat,
vegetables,
dessert—all
turned to gold.
None could
be eaten.

"Bring me food I can eat!" shouted King Midas, pushing aside his servants. They instantly turned to gold. It was not long before every piece of furniture and every living thing in the king's palace were gold—even the mice! King Midas was in despair.

"Why did I ever ask
for such a stupid gift?" King
Midas cried. "What a fool I am!"
His teardrops turned to gold and
bounced harshly on the golden floor.

To find out how to change his gift, King
Midas consulted an oracle, a priestess through
whom the gods speak.

The priestess said, "Bathe in the waters of the River
Pactolus and the curse of gold will be lifted."

King Midas ran to the River Pactolus and jumped into the water. Instantly, the river gleamed with the gold the king had shed. And the curse was lifted. When he returned to his palace, King Midas found everything as it had been before he had his golden touch. And he was happy.

He prayed to the great gods in
the sky and the winds, in the seas and
the mountains. He prayed for wisdom
and power, knowledge and generosity, and
moderation in all his ways.

And the gods listened.

And how did King Midas get rid
of his donkey ears? Well, that's
another story.

FOR
ALL THE
GOLDEN HEARTED

Margaret K. McElderry Books   An imprint of Simon &
Schuster Children's Publishing Division   1230 Avenue of the
Americas New York, New York 10020 Copyright © 2002 by Demi
All rights reserved, including the right of reproduction
in whole or in part in any form.   Book design by Michael Nelson
The text of this book is set in Elysium.   The illustrations were rendered
in paint and ink.   Printed in Hong Kong   First Edition
2   4   6   8   10   9   7   5   3   1
LIBRARY OF CONGRESS CATALOGING-IN-PUBLICATION DATA
Demi.   King Midas : the golden touch / Demi.   p. cm.   Summary:
A king finds himself bitterly regretting the consequences of
his wish that everything he touches would turn to gold.
ISBN 0-689-83297-4   1. Midas (Legendary character)—
Juvenile literature. [1.Midas (Legendary character)
2. Mythology, Greek.] I. Title. BL820.M55
D46 2001   398.2'0938'02—dc21
99-089389